JEREMY

Based on *The Railway Series* by the Rev. W. Awdry

Illustrations by
Robin Davies and Jerry Smith

EGMONT

EGMONT

We bring stories to life

First published in Great Britain in 2008
by Egmont UK Limited
239 Kensington High Street, London W8 6SA

Thomas the Tank Engine & Friends™

CREATED BY BRITT ALLCROFT

Based on the Railway Series by the Reverend W Awdry
© 2008 Gullane (Thomas) LLC. A HIT Entertainment company.
Thomas the Tank Engine & Friends and Thomas & Friends are trademarks of Gullane (Thomas) Limited.
Thomas the Tank Engine & Friends and Design is Reg. U.S. Pat. & Tm. Off.

HiT entertainment

ISBN 978 1 4052 3782 6
3 5 7 9 10 8 6 4 2
Printed in Italy

The Forest Stewardship Council (FSC) is an international, non-governmental organisation
dedicated to promoting responsible management of the world's forests. FSC operates a
system of forest certification and product labelling that allows consumers to identify
wood and wood-based products from well-managed forests.

For more information about Egmont's paper-buying policy please visit www.egmont.co.uk/ethicalpublishing

For more information about the FSC please visit their website at www.fsc.org

TO THE TRAINS ➡

This is a story about Jeremy, a splendid jet plane, who landed at Sodor Airport on the day of the summer picnic. Thomas was jealous of Jeremy until a rain storm broke out on the Island . . .

Thomas the Tank Engine loves having buffers that biff and a boiler that bubbles.

He loves having wheels that whizz round and round and a whistle that he can peep . . .

But most of all Thomas loves working on The Fat Controller's Railway.

It was the day of the Sodor Summer Picnic.

The Fat Controller came with news of a special job for Thomas. "You are to collect the children from the Airport, and take them to the picnic," he boomed, cheerfully.

Thomas was excited! "Yes, Sir," he whistled, and set off straight away.

The Airport was new and all the engines wanted to go there.

Thomas had just arrived, when he heard a loud noise in the sky. "Whoosh!"

A jet plane was coming in to land!

Thomas chuffed over to the big hangar. "Hello," he peeped. "I'm Thomas, and I'm a tank engine."

"Hello," said the plane. "I'm Jeremy and I'm a jet plane. Flying is the most fun in the world – I can see the whole Island at once," he said.

Thomas thought Jeremy was being boastful. "Well, I like travelling on tracks," he huffed.

Thomas puffed sadly away. "I never want to talk to a jet plane again!" he moaned.

He cheered up, though, when he saw the children waiting on the platform.

The Fat Controller and Lady Hatt were there, too, with a large hamper, full of delicious things to eat.

The Guard loaded the hamper into Clarabel.

Thomas set off for the picnic, but soon had to stop at a signal.

He heard Jeremy taking off. "Whoosh!"

Then Jeremy flew right over his funnel!

"It's not fair!" puffed Thomas. "Jet planes don't have to stop at signals."

At the picnic, everyone was soon having a jolly time. Everyone except Thomas.

Percy saw that he looked sad. "What's wrong, Thomas?" he asked.

"Jet planes can go wherever they like. I wish I were a jet plane," chuffed Thomas.

"But engines can pull carriages, and take children to picnics," peeped Percy. "Engines are Really Useful!"

Thomas wasn't so sure.

Jeremy was jetting to the Mainland, but dark rain clouds were gathering. Jeremy had to return to the Airport.

Thomas was passing, as Jeremy came in to land. Thomas didn't want to talk to him.

"Thomas!" Jeremy called out. "A summer storm is on its way, the picnic will be ruined!"

"Cinders and ashes!" gasped Thomas. "I must tell The Fat Controller."

Thomas steamed through tunnels and whizzed round bends. He reached the picnic just as the first drops of rain began to fall.

"Quickly!" he whooshed. "A big storm is coming. The picnic will be washed away!"

Everyone helped pack up the picnic and boarded Annie and Clarabel.

The children were sad that the picnic was over. Then Thomas had an idea. He steamed to the Airport, as fast as his wheels would carry him.

Jeremy was inside keeping nice and dry in his big hangar.

"Please can the children have their picnic here in your hangar?" asked Thomas.

"Of course," said Jeremy. "What a splendid idea!"

Thomas was very happy.

Soon, all the children were feeling jolly again. And so was The Fat Controller.

"Well done, Thomas and Jeremy!" he boomed. "Together you have saved the picnic. You are both Really Useful!"

Jeremy was happy to have helped.

And Thomas had never felt prouder to be a tank engine.

Now, whenever Thomas sees Jeremy flying high above him in the sky, he always whistles, "peep, peep!".

And Jeremy likes nothing better than looking out for Thomas, steaming along his branch line on the Island of Sodor.

The Thomas Story Library is THE definitive collection of stories about Thomas and ALL his friends.

5 more Thomas Story Library titles will be chuffing into your local bookshop in 2009!

Stanley
Flora
Colin
Hank
Madge

And there are even more Thomas Story Library books to follow late

So go on, add to your Thomas Story Library NOW!

A Fantastic Offer for Thomas the Tank Engine Fans!

STICK POUND COIN HERE

In every Thomas Story Library book like this one, you will find a special token. Collect 6 Thomas tokens and we will send you a brilliant Thomas poster, and a double-sided bedroom door hanger! Simply tape a £1 coin in the space above, and fill out the form overleaf.

TO BE COMPLETED BY AN ADULT

To apply for this great offer, ask an adult to complete the coupon below
and send it with a pound coin and 6 tokens, to:
THOMAS OFFERS, PO BOX 715, HORSHAM RH12 5WG

☐ Please send a Thomas poster and door hanger. I enclose 6 tokens
plus a £1 coin. (Price includes P&P)

Fan's name..

Address...

....Postcode............................

Date of birth..

Name of parent/guardian..

Signature of parent/guardian..